to my sister

ISBEN-13: 978-0-9855399-0-0

Published by Zayandeh Publications, New York City

Printed in United Stats of America

ZAYANDEH PUBLICATIONS

Book 1

birth

Chronicles of Seemorgh & The Three Warriors

Inspired by:
The Book of Kings, epic poem by Ferdowsi Toosi

by Mariam Touzie

I wish to extend my gratitude to my friends who supported and advised me:
Nilou Safavieh for designing, Maryam Pirnazar, Mehrdad Jamei and Leyla Ebtehadj
for editing, and Beth Bartholomew for her endless contributions. Without their help
I would not have been able to complete this book.

Birth is the story of the great warrior, Saum.

When the woman he loves dies at childbirth Saum forsakes his newborn son because the baby looks strange. Living a solitary life, Saum remains loyal to his King and protects the land.

Years go by and Saum has dreams that begin to guide him. Through symbols and signs he is led to a search for the child he once disowned, only to find that the child has been saved by the mythical bird, Seemorgh.

Birth is one of many timeless stories in *The Book of Kings*.

Although these tales describe events believed to have happened thousands of years ago in Iran, I invite you to see beyond time and place, to discover Saum the warrior, and to follow his amazing journey. You may come to agree with me that Ferdowsi's tale is profoundly relevant to our times, for it speaks of the many battles we must wage against our worst fears and deepest prejudices.

I believe every angle of this story is an invitation to open a new door and rediscover our forgotten human powers.

Characters (in order of appearance)

 Midwife

 King Manoochehr: Successor to the throne.

 Saum: Greatest among the warriors of the kingdom and father of Zal.

  Prince Nozar and **his younger brother**: Sons of King Manoochehr.

 Mother of Zal: Gives b rth to the most amazing baby boy.

 Zal: Son of Saum.

Seemorgh: A mytholoçica bird in ancient Iran.

It happened thousands of years ago in Iran,
in the state of Zabolestan, at the heart of the country...

The midwife arrives at Saum's mansion.

Saum the Warrior is at the King Manoochehr's coronation ceremony.

The warrior returns home to find the beautiful woman he loves lying lifeless in her bed.

Meanwhile the midwife presents him with a child whom he could never have imagined as his.

A giant albino!

Saum is petrified.

"He is

...too big!

...too old!

...not mine!

...not hers!
She is the most beautiful woman in the world.

He is not human.

Is this a demon?!

Take him away, far away, to the northern mountains!!!"
—Saum the father

Sorrowful servants reluctantly take son of Saum to the Alborz mountains.

The newborn Zal cries. He is alone in the mountains. Seemorgh the magnificent bird hears him at the summit, and her heart trembles. She flies over to him and picks him up, knowing this is not a prey but a precious child to be raised with her own.

Years pass

During which Saum the Warrior gains much honor.
He triumphs in many battles, defeats demons, and slays dragons.

The king, the princes, and his fellow citizens all adore him.

He remains a widower and father to no one.

Dream 1

One night in a dream Saum is visited by a Hindu.

The warrior is shaken by the dream.

The sighting

A caravan of merchants travelling from the north finds a boy roaming about with wild animals, high up in the mountains.

Saum the Warrior gathers together all his sage friends and
tells them of his dream and the sighting too.

The friends consult among themselves before advising:
"Seek your forsaken child."

Dream 2

Three men appear with a book. They talk to the warrior about the wisdom of the majestic bird. One of them questions the bravery of the warrior.

Saum contemplates.

Now he begins to see past the fog of fear, arrogance, and prejudice. He is able to think of the baby – any baby – facing wolves, lions, or even lesser animals in the mountains.

How could his child have survived for a day, a night, or even an hour?

The warrior leaves his mansion. His friends accompany him.

They ride to the edge of Alborz mountains. There, horses can no longer pass.

Saum goes on foot.

He circles the mountains over and over again to find a way to the summit.
There is none! He tries to make his own path but achieves just a little.

Then he stops all challenges. He kneels to speak to his creator.

At the summit of Alborz mountains lives Seemorgh and her children with her adopted human child Zal, son of Saum the Warrior. She now has an understanding of Saum – she knows his sorrows, his desires, and also his sincerity.

The divine bird gives two of her feathers to Zal, saying: "Burn one of these if you ever need me, and I will appear in the blink of an eye. Your father is here and you are going to live among your own kind soon."

Zal, wild and amazed, arrives with the only parent he knows.
An unspeakable joy comes over the mountains and all who are there.

Full of appreciation, Saum the Warrior receives his son Zal.

He praises Seemorgh for her wisdom and love. The divine bird trusts that Zal will grow
to be a warrior, a warrior who is both wise and skillful.

Zal, who had never tasted his mother's milk, allows himself to embrace his father's love.

Going home.

Grateful Saum promises his son:
I will comply with your every wish from now on.

33

King Manoochehr sends his first son Prince Nozar to invite Saum and Zal to the palace. And welcomes Zal in the most regal fashion, showering him with many gifts.

Zal accepts his new life with grace.

The End

Mariam Touzie was born in Tehran, Iran. She graduated
from Tehran University in Fine Arts. She then moved to
New York City, continuing her studies at the School
of Visual Arts where she received her masters degree
and was awarded the Paula Rhodes prize for exquisite
artwork. She published Rostam the Warrior in 2009.
www.mariamtouzie.blogspot.com

www.ingramcontent.com/pod-product-compliance
Lightning Source LLC
Chambersburg PA
CBHW041930010726
47507CB00003BA/233